ALICE OSEMAN

HEARTSTOPPER

HODDER CHILDREN'S BOOKS

First published in 2021 by Hodder and Stoughton

17

Text and illustrations copyright © Alice Oseman, 2021

This comic is drawn digitally using a Wacom Intuos Pro tablet directly into Photoshop CC.

A CIP catalogue record for this book
is available from the British Library.

ISBN 978 1 444 95279 7
WTS ISBN 978 1 444 96306 9

Printed and bound in Great Britain by
Clays Ltd, Elcograf S.p.A

The paper and board used in this book
are made from wood from responsible sources.

MIX
Paper from
responsible sources
FSC® C104740

Hodder Children's Books
An imprint of
Hachette Children's Group
Part of Hodder and Stoughton
Carmelite House
50 Victoria Embankment
London EC4Y 0DZ

An Hachette UK Company
www.hachette.co.uk

www.hachettechildrens.co.uk

www.aliceoseman.com

CONTENTS

CONTENT WARNING:
Please be aware that this volume of Heartstopper
contains depictions of mental health issues, including
anorexia and self-harm. For a more detailed description
of this content, please visit:
aliceoseman.com/content-warnings

✱ Not caught up with the story so far?
Read chapters 1 & 2 in *VOLUME 1!*
Read chapter 3 in *VOLUME 2!*
Read chapter 4 in *VOLUME 3!*

5. LOVE

So tell him, then.

It- it's not that easy!!!

?

It's probably too early. And if he doesn't feel the same, it'll just make things weird.

And I don't want him to do the awkward "I love you too" thing just because he feels obligated to say it back.

LEAN

917

920

If Nick joins our family then I'll have TWO big brothers and that's more than anyone in my class!

Charlie! Nick's here to pick you up!

Okay! Just coming!

GRAB

923

928

chatter

chatter

PULL

CAUGHT

933

934

937

940

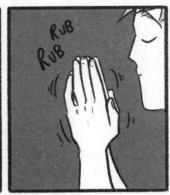

Nick! Stop kissing your boyfriend and HURRY UP!

PFFT

STAND

RUB

Haven't you seen him shirtless like a hundred times in the changing room at rugby practice?

This is an _entirely_ different context!!

946

You took your hair down.

Yeah? So?

Looks nice

You're still not allowed any snacks until lunch time.

You literally just offered Charlie some!

He's not feeling great. He's allowed some.

Charlie?

Maybe in a bit. Thanks though.

CRISPS

SPLASH

!!

I'm not going any further in. It's too cold.

SPLASH

DARCY!!

You're welcome ü

You're lucky I love you

AAH the donut's floating away

GRAB IT!!

A few weeks ago...

TAP

TAP

TAP

TAP

956

957

FORMING A PLAN.

Pfft

Oh hi there

Hi

Wanna go somewhere else to eat?

Thanks

It's okay

969

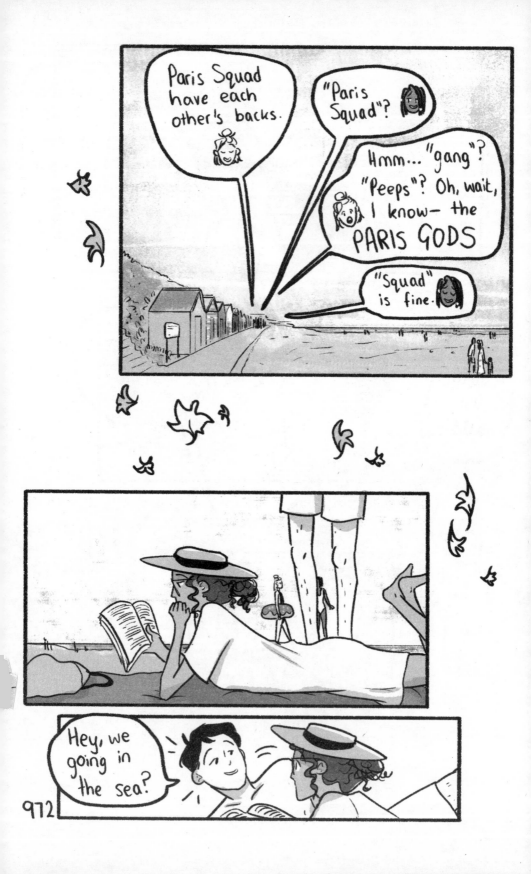

You know I don't have a swimsuit.

We could just paddle?

Fine. ♡

975

979

985

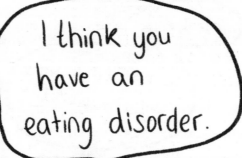

I think you have an eating disorder.

I've been doing some research and I know you don't want me to, like, try to cure you, but I care about you so much and I can see how much worse it's gotten over the pa—

Most people think eating disorders are ... a girl thing.

But they're not! I looked it up! We can show your parents articles and websites about it!

We can explain and- and then they can help!

Yeah, we could try.

CRUNCH

munch munch

ARGH

I'm leaving for Menorca in twelve hours and I CAN'T FIND MY GOGGLES!!

SNUGGLE

You **know** I'm gonna miss you a lot.

KISS

HA HA

Okay, I need to shower. I can still feel sand everywhere.

ROLL

Nick's so in love with you it's a little unbearable to watch sometimes.

1005

...what d'you mean?

When you asked me whether the eating thing was what I wanted to talk to you about. That wasn't actually what I was gonna talk to you about.

I was actually gonna say...

1012

THUNDER

RUMBLE

ZOOM

WHAT are you doing, young man?

WHERE DID CHARLIE GO?

He said he had to go home. Why?

1017

It's embarrassing

Want me to say it first, then?

Uh, I definitely said it first, I'm not letting you have this one!!

HA HA HA!

1023

1026

hi

i love you

a lot

 HI I love you too

I LOVE YOU!!! I like saying it

I miss you so much already

are you even at the airport yet lol

 ....no

 My little cousins say hi!!!

omg

can i come to menorca with you pls

 Plane leaves in 90 mins!

Can you run that fast??

i could try

i could fit in your suitcase

 We've landed!!

 come back

Are you gonna talk to your parents about the eating thing?

i'll try xx

 ♡♡♡♡

♡♡♡♡♡♡♡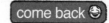

Nick?

Charlie!! Hi!

I'm so sorry, there's no phone signal or wifi at our villa, I had to walk into town.

Ch----- so----
phone ~-~--
~-w ~-
~-the ~-

Nick ~---- ~~
~can't ~--
bad signal ~-
~- --

The first week.

The second week.

Hey!! How's your day??? 😊

Hey

You've barely said a word tonight...

You okay?

Just missing Nick, or...

Is there something else?

1051

The third week.

Tori! You couldn't have dressed up a bit for dinner? Your grandparents have come all the way from the south of Spain!

...I think I look fine.

EYE ROLL

Just go and fetch your brothers, please! They'll be here soon!

knock knock

Charlie?

¡Hola, abuelo!

¡Charlie! ¿Cómo te va en el colegio?

¿B-bien?

PAT PAT

Ah, they are still not teaching you good Spanish at that school!

Is something wrong, Charlie?

I- yeah- sorry- I don't feel well... um... I'll be back in a minute

Nick Nelson

message   co

1056

1071

He needs help from a doctor or a therapist—

Someone who knows about eating disorders and how to treat them.

Love can't cure a mental illness.

But also knowing that...
sometimes people need more support than just one person can give.

You love him very much, don't you.

NOD NOD

How about we make a plan:

FFSSSH

 i can't wait to see you at school tomorrow!!!!!!!!

1082

Same!!!!!!! I MISS YOU

!! i?! !!?

Get me the fuck out of here.

You mean you actually <u>want</u> to go back to school?

Literally anywhere's better than this house.

Nick!

CHRISTIAN
OTIS
SAI

Jesus, Nick, where have you been all summer?

Innit, I feel like you just disappeared!

Oh, yeah, well I was in Menorca for like three weeks, so...

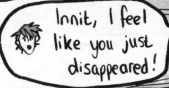

So it's nothing to do with the fact that you have a BOYFRIEND.

Oh, we're just putting that out there, then.

So... you guys heard about me and Charlie?

I mean... I think everyone in our year knows.

Sorry if we made you feel awkward about telling us.

Your "good mates" comment probably didn't help.

That was ONE TIME.

When will you stop bringing that up?

1093

SQUEEZE

1095

Missed you

Welcome back
Hamlet 5!

Zzz

If you're worried about a loved one

It can be difficult to bring up the topic of mental health, even with those closest to us. You may be worried about saying the wrong thing or upsetting the person in question. But breaking the silence can be the first important step towards recovery.

Here are some tips for talking to a loved one about their mental health:

Okay class!

1107

Saturday

FLATTEN

ew

HAPPY BIRTHDAY

DRRRINNNG

It's fine, I don't really care...

Well, we're still gonna have a super fun birthday afternoon

1111

There's an actual present in the bottom of the bag.

... Don't judge my wrapping skills

h-huh?

Char... you said wake you up at eight

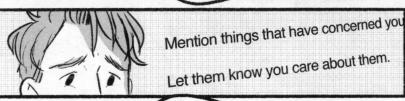

Mention things that have concerned you

Let them know you care about them.

NOD
NOD

If they acknowledge that they need help, encourage the person to seek it as soon as possible.

What if my parents say I'm faking it, or— or they get angry—

What if I came with you? I dunno... just to hold your hand? They probably wouldn't get angry if I was there!

NOD NOD

Um, also... I read online that sometimes it's easier to write it down?

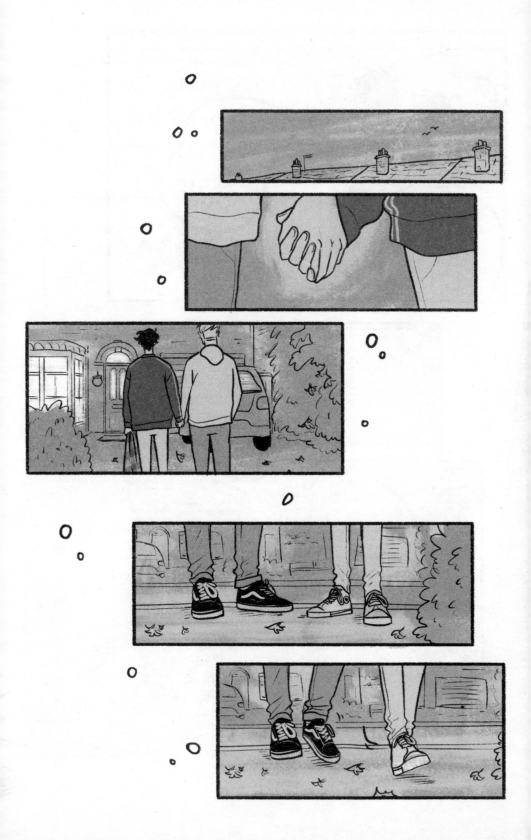

I...

...need to talk to you about something.

What's up?

Um... well...

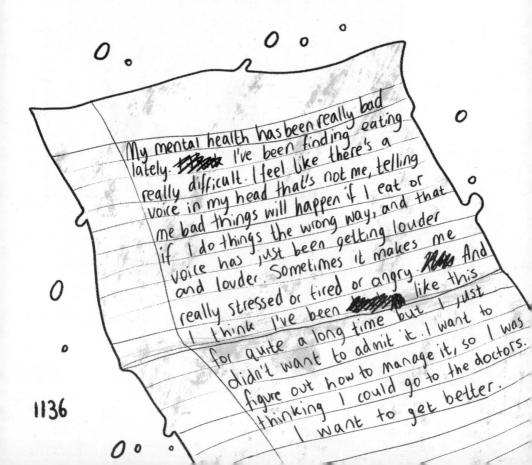

6. JOURNEY

December 31st

So... I haven't written anything for a while. The past few months have been stressful, but... I think things are looking up?

1143

Although— you know that saying that things sometimes get worse before they get better?

Yeah. I think I understand that now.

So back in September, Charlie got a GP appointment.

9:15a.m.? Great, thank you.

SUCCESS!!

He said he hates going to the doctor for anything. I mean, I can relate.

But this was extra scary.

For obvious reasons.

The doctor was helpful, and referred Charlie to an eating disorder service, but the waiting list was <u>so long</u>.

His first appointment wasn't until

January.

And things started to get

really bad after that.

But things just got harder for him.
There was one night in October
where his parents had to take him to A&E.

He knew the compulsions made no sense.
But he didn't know how to stop them.

Neither did I.

Charlie's mental health was assessed while he was there, and they told him that it'd be best if he spent some time as an inpatient.

But it was his choice.

Mental Health Treatment In Hospital

Most treatment for mental illnesses is done outside hospital. However, if you are experiencing a mental health crisis, staying in hospital may be the best way to keep you safe and provide you with the treatment you need.

While each hospital is different, this leaflet will give you an overview of what to expect:

- Why might I need to go to hospital?
- How do I access hospital treatment?
- How do I prepare for a hospital stay?
- Can I be forced to go to hospital?
- What happens inside a psychiatric hospital?
- What types of wards are there?
- What happens when I leave?

More information: mind.org.uk

Charlie said yes.

It was weird
being at school without Charlie.
I couldn't stop worrying about him.

We spoke on the phone when we could, and obviously I visited a lot too, but—

I kept wishing I knew how he was feeling all the time.

Was he homesick?

Was the treatment helping?

Was it making things worse?

Was he lonely?

Was he bored?

Had he made some friends?

What is it like in a psychiatric hospital?

Your experience can depend on the hospital you stay at, what kind of treatment you receive, and your feelings about being in hospital.

However, some common aspects of psychiatric hospitals include:
- access to talking therapies and medication
- trained staff on site to support you
- a daily routine/structure

There are also some potential disadvantages:
- you will be away from family and friends, and visits might only be permitted at set times
- you can't always decide how you spend your time
- staff may need to search you if they

It feels so awful to complain about my feelings when Charlie's been going through all of that, but I guess I've been pretty anxious these past few months.

But I talk to Mum about it a lot. That helps.

Charlie asked me not to tell them what was going on with him.

He was kinda scared of it spreading around school.

They knew he was off school because he was unwell, though, so they've been supportive in their own way.

Charlie said I could keep the
Paris Squad updated.

 Elle Argent
darcy did you get the card for charlie?

 Darcy Olsson
YEP i got a giant one, it's the length of my arm

 Tara Jones
omg

 Tao Xu
Nick does Charlie have access to a DVD player???
I was thinking we could send him some fun films to watch

Nick Nelson
yeah he does!!! Good idea, he literally said
they don't have Netflix or anything and
they've only got movies from like 2005 haha

 Tara Jones
I got the gift basket! And some
stickers and stuff to make it pretty

 Aled Last
i got him some art stuff!

 Sahar Zahid
I got him a couple of books!! He said he
likes to read so I hope that's okay

Nick Nelson
Do you all wanna come back to mine after school
tomorrow?? You can sign the card and we can
decorate the gift basket and stuff! also you can
come on a walk with Nellie and me if you want!!

 Darcy Olsson
I WOULD LIKE TO MEET NELLIE

 Elle Argent
i also would like to meet nellie!!!!

 Tao Xu
I think we all would like to meet Nellie tbh

He didn't want them all visiting — I think
it would have been too overwhelming.
But they still found ways to help.

1158

I'd go with Charlie's family to visit him a couple of times a week.

Part of me wished I could go every day, but he needed space.

I got to know Tori and Oliver pretty well during all the long car journeys.

Tori's kind of quiet, but I think she likes me? I dunno.

She's kind of... intense.

It took a few weeks, and a lot of visits, but Charlie started to seem a little better.

Staying in a hospital was a big risk. It probably isn't helpful for everyone.

But it was for him.

He could actually focus on his mental health without worrying about school and what everyone thought.

He came
home in
early
December.

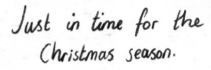

Just in time for the Christmas season.

He's still dealing with a lot, so he stayed off school for the rest of term.

Christmas Day was especially hard. He came round mine after a big argument with his mum.

He got to meet our new puppy,
Henry, which cheered him up
a bit, but...

It was
a difficult day.

It's not like seven weeks in hospital made him magically okay again.

I know I'm not an expert or anything, but from what I've learnt over the past few months, mental illnesses take a long time to go away completely... if they ever do.

This is probably only the start of a long journey.

But he's definitely doing better.

He's having therapy sessions with this guy called Geoff.

He hasn't self-harmed since October.

And he's been thinking differently about how to deal with his anorexia.

We've been messaging a lot while I'm at school.

Tao's been bringing him all the work he's missed.

Yesterday we were just hanging out in his room...

and he said something funny

and we just started laughing

and couldn't stop for ages

1170

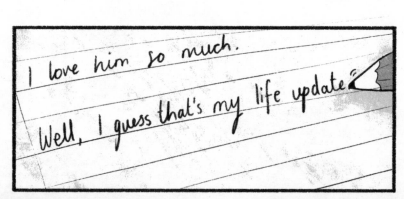

I love him so much.

Well, I guess that's my life update?

Scribble

Scribble

Anyway, I'd better go — Charlie will be here soon! We're going to a New Year's Eve party tonight!

A guy in my year is having a big house party with fireworks and stuff.

It's the first time Charlie will have been back with a bunch of people from school. We can always leave if it's awful, but I'm excited.

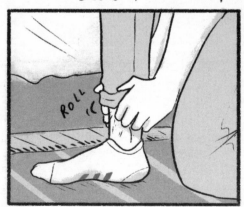

Ready!

I'm excited to just hang out at a party with my boyfriend.

Are you sure you don't mind... um... people seeing...?

Char. Everyone knows we're dating.

Yeah, but you only came out to school people a few months ago...

It was five months ago. Stop worrying about me.

WAIT—

1183

MARCH

But I haven't written in here since last summer, and a lot has happened since then.

I can't believe I've been having therapy for like four months already.

I hated the idea at first.

Even though I admitted I needed it.

And things didn't exactly get off to a great start, what with the waiting time, and me just spiralling after that.
If you feel you may be su
rom mental health problems, seek
ofessional help as soon as possibl
ppointment date: Tuesday 4th Januar
ou need to
et out of bed
and stop
eing so lazy
e are you off school agai
Are you feeling ok? I can se
you the maths homework b
it's due tomorrow and Mr S
d if you don't ha
does charlie read the group
chat?? where is he??
ou keep ski
meals, you're
even tr
isgusting
harlie please message m
m so worried about you!!!
don't deserv
“Mental health waiting times
children and teens ‘dangerous
nd unhelpful’”
uiry into the latest waiting
need to stay
in control or ever
bad an
Things got bad really fast.

Spending a few weeks in a psych ward was obviously not my plan.

And there were some ups and downs there, sure.

But I think I got lucky because the place I went to was actually helpful. 1195

I started therapy there. Not with Geoff, but the therapist was really nice.

I had a nutritionist, too. I know that isn't the case for all psych wards.

We weren't allowed mobile phones, but I could still call home from the ward phone.

Some of the rules kinda sucked, and some days were awful, but a lot of it was fine. I even made a couple of friends.

At first, I think there was a big part of me that didn't even want to get better. That just wanted to keep pretending I was fine, so I didn't have to put in the effort to change.

I was so scared of losing control.

Eating was something I could control.

Being in hospital didn't make me completely free of mental illness. Not even close.

But it got me out of the deep end.

Geoff is my therapist now that I'm back home.

Me and Geoff have talked about what's happened in my life over the past couple of years.

It's weird. I knew that bad things had happened—

Getting outed.

The bullying.

Ben.

But I hadn't processed any of it. I hadn't realised it had all affected me so much.

Geoff says it's trauma.

Kind of a dramatic word, I guess, but Geoff says trauma can come from all sorts of things.

Geoff says I'm making progress, but I think I'm realising now that there might never be an "end".

But Geoff also says the bad days will get less common. And I can just enjoy my life and hardly ever stress out about food.

Some days I think he's full of shit.

But some days I feel hopeful. I guess I'll have to keep trying.

So I went back to school after the Christmas holidays!

A couple of teachers knew what had happened.

Mr Farouk and Miss Singh have been really supportive.

Especially as rugby has been kinda hard.

I think Tori feels guilty about everything.

She shouldn't, but...

her mental health hasn't been great either.

But she's made this new friend called Michael.

But really.

I had a self-harm relapse in mid-January.

Me and Nick were eating dinner at mine, and we just got into a silly little argument.

We were both tired and stressed, and I'd had a really bad day so I was being shitty.

He left, and... yeah.

I just got the urge.

It wasn't anyone's fault. Relapses happen.
Tori told Nick what had happened, and
he came back later that night.

We
made
up.

Mum and Dad even let him stay over
to "keep an eye on me".

Not really necessary, but I wasn't complaining.

Nick?

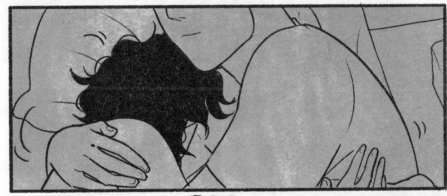

I love Nick.

I love Nick so, so much.

But what I've realised through all of this is that we need other people too.

Siblings.

Parents.

Friends.

More friends.

A therapist.

Even teachers, sometimes.

That doesn't mean our relationship
isn't strong.

If anything...

I think
we're stronger
now.

I know big dinners aren't your fave.

Yeah, I'll be okay. I've planned what I'm having. And I want to be there for Nick. He hasn't seen his dad for like a year, so he's pretty nervous.

He's not out to him yet, is he?

No, I think he wants to do it tonight.

You okay, darling?

I know you don't see him much, but... it's only your dad.

I don't know why he insists on these big dinners whenever he comes here but I'm sure it'll be fine.

I think I'm gonna come out to him.

1223

Hi

Hi

Do we need to pretend to be platonic BFFs in front of your dad?

I mean... yeah, maybe just until I talk to him about us...

But— are you gonna be okay with dinner—

Nick.

I'm gonna be fine.

Let me worry about you this time.

PEEK

inhale
exhale

You okay?

1238

Nick—

You're just gonna let him talk to me like that!?

Be quiet David. We've heard enough from you!

... You have not grown up into the man I had hoped you would be, David.

1239

SIT

Are you okay?

Nicky...

I knew something would go wrong this evening

...sorry

No, I'm glad you said what you said. Especially to your dad. He needed to hear it.

Want me to talk to him for you?

1243

No, I... I want to talk to him.

Properly.

[Leaving, then?] [in French]

Nicholas... [I'm sorry.]

[I was happy to meet your fr- your boyfriend.]

[I don't really... understand these things. But he seems like a very nice young man.]

[He is.]

[I'm not going back to Paris until next Friday...]

1247

CREAK

KICK

Me and Nick thought — like, since he passed his test — we'd go out for a drive?

Maybe, like, to the arcade, or... I think the milkshake café stays open late...?

I promise I'll only be an hour or two—

1258

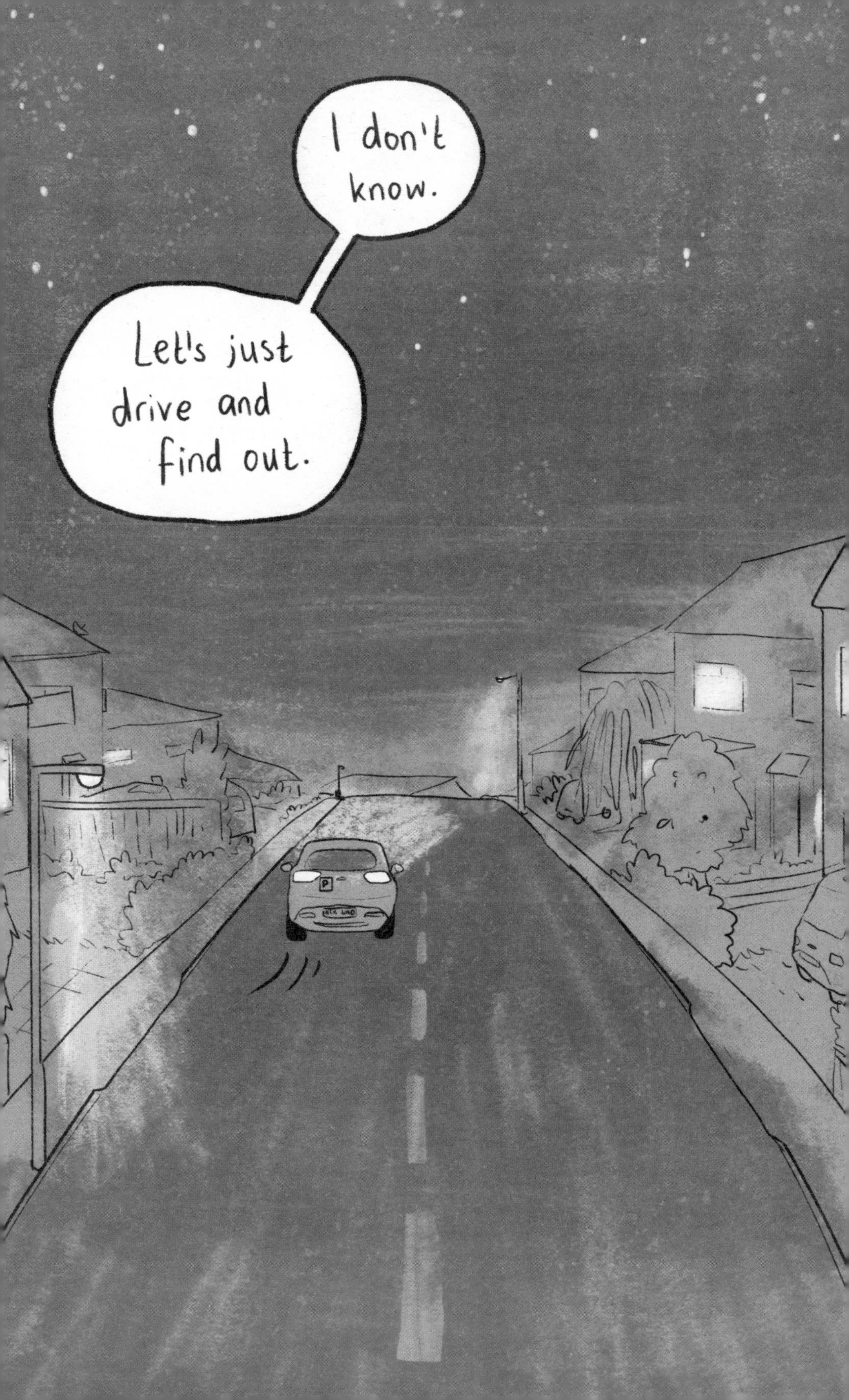
I don't know.
Let's just drive and find out.

Heartstopper will continue in
Volume 5!

Read more of the comic online:

heartstoppercomic.tumblr.com
tapas.io/series/heartstopper

Firsts

A HEARTSTOPPER MINI-COMIC

FIRST KISS

FIRST WEEKEND AWAY

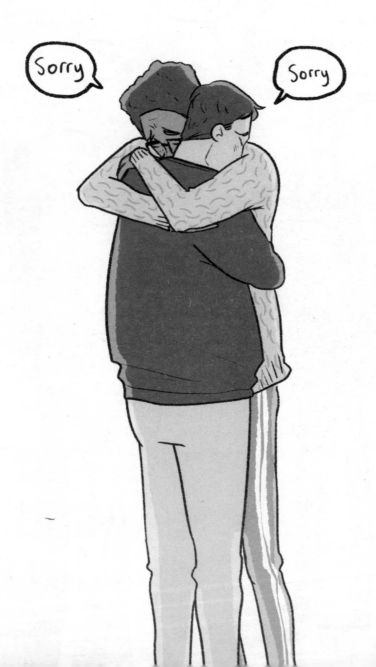

NAME: CHARLES "CHARLIE" SPRING

WHO ARE YOU: NICK'S BOYFRIEND

SCHOOL YEAR: YEAR 11   **AGE:** 15

BIRTHDAY: APRIL 27TH

MBTI: ISTP

FUN FACT: I LOVE TO READ!

NAME: Nicholas "Nick" Nelson

WHO ARE YOU: Charlie's boyfriend

SCHOOL YEAR: Year 12   **AGE:** 17

BIRTHDAY: September 4th

MBTI: ESFJ

FUN FACT: I'm great at baking cakes

NAME: Tao Xu

WHO ARE YOU: Charlie's friend

SCHOOL YEAR: Year 11   **AGE:** 16

BIRTHDAY: September 23rd

MBTI: ENFP

FUN FACT: I have a film review blog

NAME: Victoria "Tori" Spring

WHO ARE YOU: Charlie's sister

SCHOOL YEAR: Year 12   **AGE:** 16

BIRTHDAY: April 5th

MBTI: INFJ

FUN FACT: I HATE (ALMOST) EVERYONE

NAME: Elle Argent
WHO ARE YOU: Charlie's friend
SCHOOL YEAR: Year 12   **AGE:** 16
BIRTHDAY: May 4th
MBTI: ENTJ
FUN FACT: I like making clothes ♡

NAME: Tara Jones
WHO ARE YOU: Darcy's girlfriend
SCHOOL YEAR: Year 12   **AGE:** 16
BIRTHDAY: July 3rd
MBTI: INFP
FUN FACT: I love dance! (especially ballet)

NAME: Darcy Olsson
WHO ARE YOU: Tara's girlfriend
SCHOOL YEAR: Year 12   **AGE:** 17
BIRTHDAY: January 9th
MBTI: ESFP
FUN FACT: I once ate a whole jar of mustard for a dare

NAME: Aled Last
WHO ARE YOU: Charlie's friend
SCHOOL YEAR: Year 11   **AGE:** 15
BIRTHDAY: August 15th
MBTI: INFJ
FUN FACT: I want to make a Podcast

NAME:
Sarah Nelson
WHO ARE YOU:
Nick's mum

NAME:
David Nelson
WHO ARE YOU:
Nick's brother

NAME:
Sahar Zahid
WHO ARE YOU:
Tara, Darcy, &
Elle's friend

NAME:
Mr Ajayi
WHO ARE YOU:
Art teacher

NAME:
Mr Farouk
WHO ARE YOU:
Science
teacher

NAME:
Nellie
WHO ARE YOU:
Nick's dog

NAME:
JANE SPRING
WHO ARE YOU:
CHARLIE'S MUM

NAME:
Julio Spring
WHO ARE YOU:
Charlie's dad

NAME:
Oliver Spring
WHO ARE YOU:
Charlie's bro

NAME:
Stéphane Fournier
WHO ARE YOU:
Nick's dad

NAME:
Henry
WHO ARE YOU:
Nick's dog #2

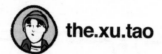

64 likes

the.xu.tao third wheeling

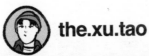

71 likes

the.xu.tao third wheel part 2 (they've been making out for like half an hour)

cfspring why are you so obsessed with me!!!!!
the.xu.tao @cfspring i just ship you two so much
cfspring @the.xu.tao fuck off

the.xu.tao

98 likes

the.xu.tao third wheel part 3. literally just trying to do my maths homework here

cfspring IT WAS JUST A PECK WE WEREN'T EVEN MAKING OUT
the.xu.tao @cfspring still inappropriate school behaviour and i will report you to the authorities
cfspring @the.xu.tao homophobia

 **cfspring**

102 likes

cfspring NOW who's the third wheel huh @**the.xu.tao**

the.xu.tao ...truce?
cfspring @**the.xu.tao** truce

Mental Health Resources

For information, help, support and guidance about mental health and mental illness, please check out the following resources:

Beat Eating Disorders –
www.beateatingdisorders.org.uk

Mind –
www.mind.org.uk

OCD UK –
www.ocduk.org

YoungMinds –
www.youngminds.org.uk

MindOut LGBTQ Mental Health Service –
www.mindout.org.uk

Rethink Mental Illness –
www.rethink.org

Switchboard LGBT+ Helpline –
switchboard.lgbt

Author's note

Hello everyone! I really hope you have enjoyed the fourth volume of Heartstopper. Can you believe we're already on the fourth volume? I certainly can't!

This volume mostly followed Charlie's mental health journey. I wanted to explore some of his struggles with his eating disorder, but to always show that recovery is possible, and that even though it may not be a straightforward journey, things can get better. But romantic love does not "cure" mental illness, as movies often suggest! This is something Nick learns in this volume. Nick can be there for him, but Charlie has to find his own path to recovery.

So much has happened since the last volume. I got to go on a UK book tour in early 2020, release a Heartstopper colouring book, and was finally able to announce that a TV adaptation is in the works with Netflix and See-Saw Films. None of this would have been possible without all you brilliant, passionate readers. I'm so, so grateful for your support and love for the series.

A huge thanks as always to the wonderful team working on Heartstopper: my amazing agent, Claire Wilson, my incredible editor, Rachel Wade, my awesome publicist, Emily Thomas, everyone at Hachette who is a part of the Heartstopper journey, and all the international publishers around the world who are now supporting the series too.

I know that many of you are sad that the next volume will be the final volume of Nick and Charlie's story. I'm sad too! But I promise that it shall be magical and heartwarming and full of queer joy.

See you in Volume Five!

Alice x

Collect the whole Heartstopper series!

Read more about Nick and Charlie...

Or read Alice's other prose fiction...

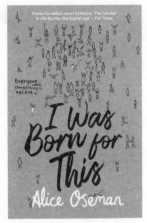